This 2010 edition licensed for publication by Sandy Creek
by arrangement with HarperCollins Publishers.

HarperCollins Publishers® and I Can Read Books® are registered trademarks.

ADVENTURES OF STUART LITTLE

Sandy Creek
122 Fifth Avenue
New York, NY 10011

ISBN-13: 978-0-7607-7111-2

Printed in China

Manufactured 04/2010

10 11 12 13 SCP 10 9 8

Stuart Hides Out

One day Stuart Little's mother,

father, and brother, George, went out.

Stuart was left alone

with the family cat, Snowbell.

“I guess it’s just you and me, Snowbell,” said Stuart.

“Oh joy,” said Snowbell.

"We could have fun together," Stuart said. "You know, like friends do."

"Please," said Snowbell.

"I don't eat you for lunch.

That is as friendly as I get

with a mouse."

"Let's play a game,"

said Stuart.

Snowbell yawned.

"Checkers? Parcheesi?"

said Stuart.

"How about a nice game

of hide-and-seek,"

Snowbell said.

"You hide, I'll seek."

"Hide-and-seek it is,"

said Stuart. "Close your eyes

and count to one hundred!"

"You bet," Snowbell said.

He closed his eyes.

He fell asleep.

Stuart tried a few hiding places.

Then he saw a flower vase

high on a shelf.

“That is a good hiding place,”

Stuart said.

He climbed up onto the shelf

and slid down into the vase.

He sat down to wait.

“Snowbell will never find me!”

Stuart said.

After a while, Stuart said,

“It’s not very comfortable in here.”

After another while, Stuart said,

“This game used to be more fun.”

Finally Stuart said,

"I think I'm the only one playing."

Stuart stretched his arms up.

He could not reach the top of the vase.

“Oh, no!” cried Stuart.

“I’m stuck in here!”

Snowbell woke up and stretched.
"I guess old Stuart
has learned a lesson.
The mouse can't win
in a cat-and-mouse game."

After a while, Snowbell said,
"I hope he doesn't hide
for too long."
After another while, Snowbell said,
"Wait. What am I doing
even thinking about the mouse?"

Finally Snowbell said,

"I've really got to get out more."

“Nobody will ever find me in here,”

Stuart said.

“I have to tip the vase over

so I can crawl out.”

Stuart began to rock back and forth.

The vase tipped to one side.

It tipped to the other side.

Then it fell over and began to roll

faster and faster toward

the edge of the shelf!

“Whoa!” Stuart cried.

“Maybe I’ll just have

a small snack before going out,”

said Snowbell.

“Help!” Stuart yelled.

Snowbell looked up

and saw the vase rolling fast.

“Stuart!” shouted Snowbell.

He jumped onto the shelf
and pounced on the vase
just in time.

Stuart crawled out of the vase.

"Snowbell, you found me!"

cried Stuart.

"Well, I wanted a snack,

and that made me think of you,"

said Snowbell.

"Thanks for saving me," Stuart said.

"Keep it to yourself, Mouse-Boy.

This kind of cat-and-mouse game

gets no respect," said Snowbell.

"No problem, Snow,"

said Stuart.

"But next time,

I get to choose the game!"

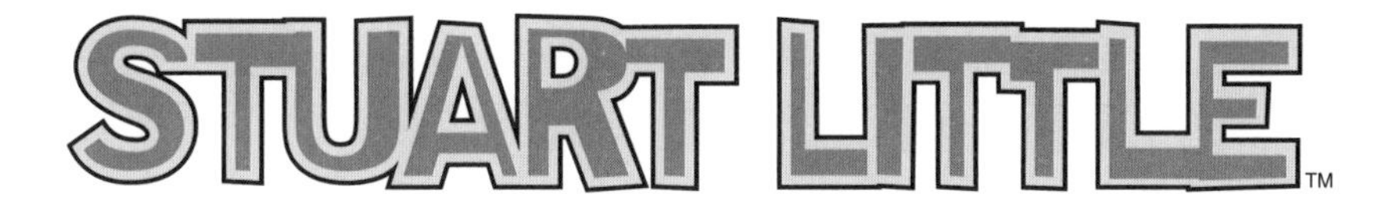
STUART LITTLE™

MAP
LAKE

Stuart Sets Sail

TO LAKE
3 miles

One sunny day,
Stuart Little and his family
drove to a lake in the country.

Mr. Little carried the picnic basket.

Mrs. Little carried the blanket.

George carried his boat, the *Wasp*.

Stuart carried dessert.

“What a big lake,” said Stuart.

“I can’t wait to sail across it!”

“That sounds like fun, Stuart,”
said Mrs. Little, “but come back
before the sun hits the tops
of those trees.
We want to be home
before it gets dark.”

Stuart set sail.

The wind blew softly.

Suddenly Stuart heard

SPLISH! SPLASH!

“It’s a whale!” Stuart yelled.

"No, I'm just a fish
with a whale of a problem.
I have a hook stuck in my lip!"
said the fish.

"I can help you," said Stuart.

He pulled the hook out.

"Thank you!" cried the fish.

"You are welcome," said Stuart.

The fish swam away.

Stuart looked up.

The sun had moved closer to the trees.

"I still have time

to cross the lake," said Stuart.

The wind picked up.

"Whooee!" shouted Stuart.

"I will be at the other side

of the lake soon!"

BUMP!

The *Wasp* ran into a rock.

"Where did that rock come from?"

asked Stuart.

He stepped onto the rock
to check for leaks in the *Wasp*.
Suddenly the rock began to move.
"Whoa!" shouted Stuart.

"Do I look like a rock to you?" it said.

"You look like a turtle, now,"

said Stuart.

"You look like lunch to me!"

snapped the turtle.

Stuart jumped back into the boat.

"Phew!" said Stuart.

"That was close!"

Stuart looked up.

The sun was closer

to the tops of the trees.

"I still have time

to cross the lake," said Stuart.

He sailed on.

Suddenly a motorboat sped by.

Big waves tossed the *Wasp*.

Then a large bird flew over the boat.

His wings whipped the sails.

“Having a good time, Sailor?”

called the bird.

"I prefer calmer winds,
if you don't mind!" Stuart shouted.
"Ha-ha." The bird laughed
and flew away.

"That was some storm!" said Stuart.

He looked up.

The sun was very close

to the tops of the trees.

The other side of the lake

was still far away.

"Well," said Stuart,

"it is time to go back."

Stuart turned the *Wasp* around

and sailed back to shore.

“Did you sail to the other side,
Stuart?” asked George.
“No,” said Stuart.
“But did you see
all my big adventures?
Did you see the fish,
the rock, and the storm?”

"We didn't see anything, Son,"
Mr. Little said.
"It looked like smooth
sailing from here."

"Oh," Stuart said. "I guess they were only little adventures."

"Adventures come in all sizes, Stuart," said Mrs. Little.

Stuart smiled.

"So does dessert!"

STUART LITTLE™

Stuart at the Library

Late one afternoon

Stuart Little went to the library.

"Do you have any books

for someone like me?"

he asked the librarian.

"How about *Mice Are Nice*,"

she said. "Third floor."

"Thanks," said Stuart.

"Is that a stuffed owl?" he asked.

“No, no. This is Bookworm.
He is our library owl.
We let him live here
because he loves books so much,”
said the librarian.

Bookworm opened one eye
and stared at Stuart.
"Owls and I don't usually get along,"
said Stuart.

“Don’t worry,” said the librarian.

“He usually sleeps

during library hours.”

“Well, thanks for the help,”

Stuart said to the librarian.

Stuart found the book.

“I’ll just read a little bit to see

if I want to borrow it,” Stuart said.

Stuart began to read.

Soon he was lost in the story.

Then he fell asleep!

Mice are Nice

Something woke Stuart.

"I must have slept

past closing time," said Stuart.

"Indeed you have," said a voice.

“Bookworm? Is that you?”

Stuart asked.

The big owl flew out of the shadows.

“It is I,” said the owl.

"Oh dear," Stuart said,

and he began to back away.

"Never fear," said Bookworm.

"I've already had my dinner.

Besides, I want to read my books,

not chase mice."

“I love to read, too!” said Stuart.

“What’s your favorite book?”

“There have been so many,”

Bookworm said.

“*Whoo* can pick just one?”

“Pick a few, then!” said Stuart.

"Hmmm, yes, well . . ."

Bookworm pointed

to the closest book on the shelf.

"I am quite fond of this one,"

he said.

"This book?" Stuart asked.

"Yes. It is a work of art
that has great meaning to me,"
said Bookworm.

Stuart looked at the book.

"You like *Lawn Care for Dummies*?"

"Is that the title?"

Bookworm said.

"Can't you read it?" asked Stuart.

"Well, no," said Bookworm.

"And no one else can find out.

I'm afraid I'll have to eat you

after all!"

Bookworm dived for Stuart.

Stuart ran!

Bookworm chased Stuart
down the hall, around the corner,
and down the stairs.
Stuart could not escape.

Bookworm landed on top of him.
"Please, Bookworm,
let me go!" Stuart cried.
"I am sorry, my bookish friend.
My secret must stop with you!"
"Wait!" cried Stuart.
"You said you weren't hungry!"
"I'm not," said Bookworm,
"but I will be sent away
if the librarian finds out
I can't read.
I am a library owl, after all."

"I promise I won't tell anyone,"

said Stuart.

"Maybe I can help you."

"I don't need help from a mouse,"

said Bookworm.

"Now, you'd better go.

Shoo! Shoo!"

Soon Stuart went back to the library.

Bookworm opened one eye and asked,

“What are you doing here?”

“I want to help you read,” said Stuart.

“Well, don’t bother me,”

said Bookworm.

“Let me sleep.”

“When you wake up,” said Stuart,

“here are some other books

you might like.”

“Let me see those,” said Bookworm.

“What is this one about?”

“It’s about a very smart owl

who finds out

it’s never too late to learn,”

said Stuart.

“Well, if you insist,” said Bookworm.

“Why don’t you start?”

"You bet!" said Stuart.

And the two new friends

began to read together.

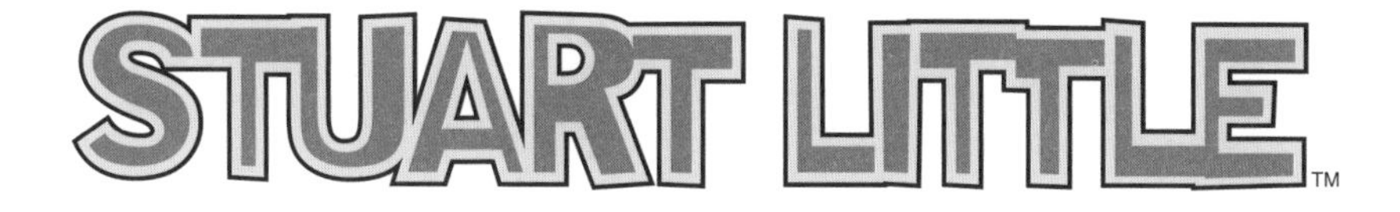
STUART LITTLE™

Stuart at the Fun House

One day

Stuart Little and his brother, George,

went to an amusement park.

RIVER PAR
ADMISSION

"Look at all the rides!"

George said.

"Look at all the food!"

Stuart said.

"This is great!" said George.

"I always wanted a brother

to go to the amusement park with."

"I'm your man!" Stuart said.

"What do you want to do first,
Stuart?" asked George.
"I want to do what you want to do,"
said Stuart.
"Look, there's the strong man game!"
said George.
"Well, I don't think . . . ,"
Stuart started to say.
But George had already run ahead.
Stuart followed.

STRONGMAN
10
9
8
7
6
5
4
3
2
1
2 Strikes 50¢

George picked up the hammer
and swung it hard.
"We have a winner!"
the man shouted.

"Your turn, Stuart," George said.

Stuart looked at the hammer.

"Do you have any other sizes?"

Stuart asked the man.

"One size fits all," the man said.

"I guess you need a strong brother

to play this game, George,"

Stuart said.

"That's okay, Stuart.
Let's try the pony ride,"
said George.

George and Stuart got on their ponies.
All the ponies began to walk
faster and faster.

Stuart's pony didn't move.

"Giddyap!" shouted Stuart.

The pony lady laughed.

"You're not heavy enough to ride!

The pony doesn't know

you're on his back," she said.

Stuart waited for George to finish.

"I guess you need a big brother

for this ride, George,"

said Stuart.

"That's okay, Stuart,"

George said.

"Let's try the roller coaster!"

ROLLER COASTER
ENTRANCE

Stuart and George stood in line for the ride.

The cars on the track looped
up and down and
around and around.
People got on and off.

"Hurray! We're finally at the front of the line," George said.

"Next!" shouted the man.

"That's us," said Stuart.

"Sorry, kid," the man said to Stuart.
He pointed at a sign.
"You must be this high
to ride the roller coaster."

"I guess you need a tall brother for this ride," said Stuart.
"You go on without me."
Stuart waited on the ground and watched George.

“Now what, Stuart?”

asked George when the ride was over.

“How about the fun house?”

“Okay,” said Stuart.

“The fun house sounds . . . fun.”

Stuart and George paid for their tickets and went inside the fun house.

A sign said:

ENTERING THE HALL OF MIRRORS.

They stepped inside.

The mirrors made them look wobbly.

The mirrors made them look wiggly.

Suddenly, they stopped

and stared.

"Look, George! I'm big now!"

Stuart said.

"And I'm small!" George said.

Big Stuart looked at little George.

Little George looked at big Stuart.

“I’m sorry I kept picking rides and games for regular-size people,” the tiny George said.

“That’s okay,” the tall Stuart said.

They stepped away from the mirrors.

"Sometimes I forget

you're not stronger, or bigger, or taller.

You're my little brother, and

you're the best brother I ever had,"

George said.

“Thanks, George,” Stuart said.

“Now you pick a ride, Stuart!”
said George.

Stuart smiled.

12